On The Bus

A SHORT STORY

Waseem Bahra

TRANSLATED BY THE AUTHOR

BAHRA BOOKS

Translation from Arabic by Waseem Bahra. First published in English by Bahra Books in 2025.

Printed in the United States of America.

For more information or to book an event, contact:

contact@bahrabooks.com

http://www.bahrabooks.com

Edited by Nicolai N. Petro

Book design by Istvan Szabo

Cover design by Lana Bahra

ISBN 979-8-218-58422-1 pbk.

First Edition: 2025

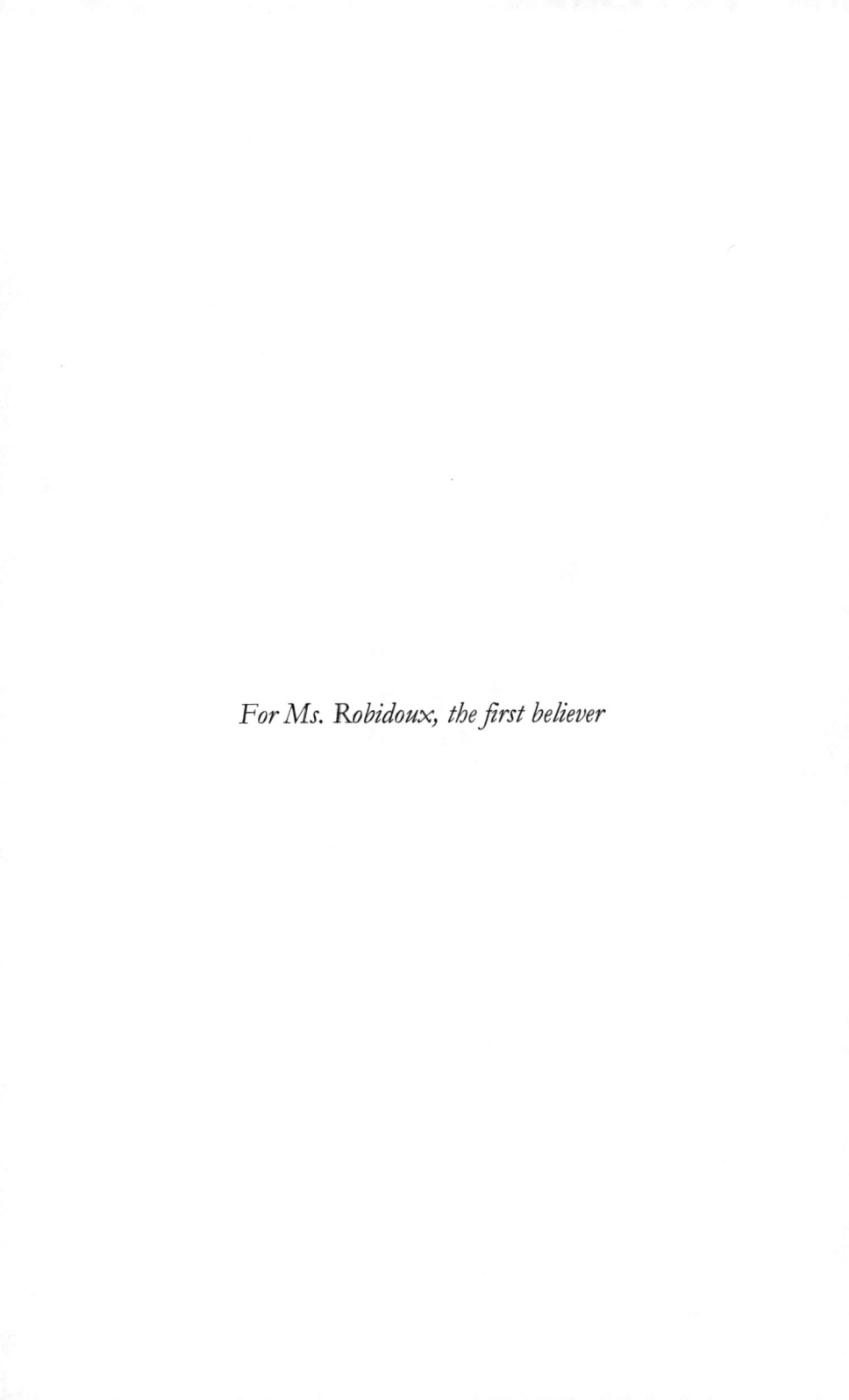

For Ms. Robidoux, the first believer

BAHRA BOOKS

All I've heard is vague tales of boats and borders.

— Yusra Mardini

BAHRA BOOKS

CHAPTER 1

TRAVELER

It was very early in the morning when I caught the bus. Afraid I wouldn't make it on time, I left my hotel room an hour early. I took the most circuitous route to the bus stop. Call me old-fashioned, but I find relying on my instincts at the pitch of stress to be much more reliable than aimlessly trusting my phone to lead the way.

I hadn't spoken a word to anyone on my way to the bus stop. Well, it's not like I was afforded many opportunities for conversation. For reasons unbeknownst to me, parents quickly drew their curtains shut when they saw me walking down the sidewalk. Teenagers on wooden park benches took photos of me with their phones as I passed by them. And even this one old lady hobbled to the other side of the street upon my approach as if she would rather die than suffer my fleeting presence.

The bus was crowded. I sat alone beside an emergency exit window, glancing up from my phone at the newly arrived passengers, who tried as noiselessly as possible to settle into the hard plastic seats. Unwittingly, perhaps, they avoided sitting in the middle rows.

At every stop, I didn't dare look up from my phone screen. I didn't want to risk making awkward eye-contact with any of the newly arrived passengers. I stole a glance or two at their general movements only when their backs were turned and their immediate preoccupation became their comfort.

Otherwise, I didn't care to busy myself with the strangers around me. It's not like I'm too socially inept to know how to talk with a stranger on the bus. Quite the opposite, I'm very outgoing and sociable in my free time; ask around the mosques[1] of this city if you don't believe me; any acquaintance of mine can recall a myriad of instances after Friday prayer[2] where I successfully rallied a portion of the men for a cup of tea and a game of cards at the local park. On the bus I chose—yes chose!—to withdraw into myself.

Perhaps I'm not being totally sincere with you. The social part of me, I suppose, withers before these people. Like a son's tongue crumbles to filial ash before his father. I don't know why. It's not like I have some overweening respect for them which silences me in their presence.

If anything, I would say I actually harbor some unspoken grievances about the careless ways they live their lives. They plunge into each other's beds like ravenous animals; they stuff themselves to the bursting point with beer and swine; drunk on their own imbecility, they exist within their bubble-like lives on their large island, toting the flag of liberty while their rulers divide and plunder nations abroad too small and impotent to be heard in their death throes.

They turn their proud features away from a traveler like me, effortlessly seeming to condemn the friendliness which

I prefer to invest in the locals, if only to distract them from the imminent realization that I do not belong here.

Am I wrong not to love them?

"Backdoor! Backdoor!" a raspy voice shouted behind me.

The backdoor hissed open.

Shoes clattered off the bus, making one side of the bus sway lightly as each passenger alighted onto the curb below. After the passengers had gotten off, silence hovered in the doorway, complete and undisturbed.

BAHRA BOOKS

CHAPTER 2

FROZE

The backdoor hissed shut.

A crisp breeze was expelled between the doors, slapping one side of my face. I felt refreshed and soothed. My nostrils yawned to welcome the sleepy fumes unfurling off every other unwashed head.

Prompted, I looked around. The bus lurched forward, jostling the limp passengers. Their heads bobbed with the dizzying ups and downs of the road. It seemed as if this bus ride cast a numb spell on its passengers that would dissipate only when they each got off at their respective stops.

I turned around to face the front of the bus.

Abruptly, I noticed a stocky businessman seated directly in front of me. He wore a navy-blue blazer of an academic style. Flecks of dandruff spotted his shoulders. Glancing up, I contemplated his graying afro without a thought in my mind.

When did he get here?

Before I could answer myself, a stranger appeared over his dandruff-spotted shoulders. He was a bald white man carrying black plastic bags. He swiped his bus pass under the scanner stationed beside the bus driver's seat; it beeped.

Without missing a beat, he swung his lanky build into an empty seat whose back was positioned against the tinted windows.

I didn't plan on stalking him; but some oddly magnetic quality about him encouraged me to steal glances. Was I staring at him? I didn't think so. I recalled the respectful looking-time here was only a few seconds; people prefer to be left alone; if he had caught me looking at him—thank god he didn't!—but, if he had, he could have reasonably heckled me or threatened my life.

Seriously.

I've heard disturbing stories from fellow travelers who on occasion unintentionally bother the locals here.

Suddenly fearing he might catch me staring at him, I resorted to observing his opaque reflection on the window. His reflection melded into a hand-print beside the emergency exit latch where I sat; but I could still discern his movements just fine.

With his bags propped against the seat beside him, he reached inside and pulled out a newspaper sleeve that was folded in half with a healthy-looking rubber band. He unbound the newspaper; a slim stack of lottery tickets slid onto his lap.

Picking up a lottery ticket, he ruminated over its unscratched dark purple circles. He tilted the lottery ticket from side to side under the harsh ceiling light as if his destiny was spelled somewhere on it. He placed the lottery ticket on his thigh, reaching into his black bag.

Then he… just… froze.

CHAPTER 3

WORRY

Literally, his entire body stiffened as he went to reach into the bag. His bloodshot eyes stayed open. Either my eyes were lagging or a profound realization had hit him at the most random moment.

When he would not move, I started to worry that something fatal had happened to him. I glanced around me to see if any of the passengers were seeing what I was seeing.

They were not.

Farther down the rows, a construction worker with headphones covering his ears continued to gaze out the window. Some student with sleepy eyes kept typing something on an iPad. This pair of middle-aged women chatted in hushed tones over a dozing fat paralegal who sat between them. A nurse in scrubs held her hands in her lap, staring at the floor.

What the hell's wrong with these people? Do they not see their fellow man in need? Do they not care for their own countrymen? If they don't care for one of their own, what makes me think they would care for me?

I snapped my head back at the frozen man.

He was staring at me. His mouth dangled open, forming an O with his saltine-thin, chapped lips. A small glistening bead of sweat trailed down his brow.

He stood up. His beetle black pupils looked politely furious. Composing his wrinkled face, he pointed his long index finger at me.

CHAPTER 4

N O !

He wasn't pointing at me, of course. He was singling out the construction worker who sat behind me. Perhaps he recognized his face from a stroll long ago along the pristine white sands of Trinidad.

Or perhaps the construction worker had boarded the same plane as him at one point in their itinerary lives. It was on the returning flight. By pure coincidence, they'd sat side-by-side, talking for the entire flight, privately dreading the casual moment when they would part from each other's company.

Perhaps this was all a joke—people love to joke here right?—and he just wanted to bother me because I had been bothering him with my furtive stares; and because his blood's light (as the expression goes) he will take this joke further than most by continuing to bore his eyes into my soul.

But I should breathe (am I breathing) since this is one huge misunderstanding which can be rectified by a discreet smile or by gazing out the window until he goes away. Even if he forcibly tried to pry my face towards him, I would steady my jaws like a bull, withstand his dirty fingernails clawing into my flesh.

I pointed at myself with a questioning look on my face.

He nodded.

"No," I whispered.

What happened to my voice? It was normally very loud, especially if I refused someone something.

He just kept staring at me.

"No," I repeated a little louder this time, clearing my throat afterwards, in case I'd have to speak again.

He described a sweeping motion with his index finger at something behind me.

I turned around.

Every passenger was on their feet. They were staring at me. Their lips formed a startled O. Their index fingers were raised at me. All at once, as if they had choreographed this part of the show, they pointed at my head.

"No!" I shouted with a voice lost at the bottom of a well.

Simultaneously, they nodded with one head.

I turned to the bald man, desperate.

While turning to him, I caught a glimpse of the bus driver in the wide rear-view mirror. With one eye on the rapidly descending road, his other eye fixed me with a cold stare. The rear-view mirror froze a reflection of him also pointing his index finger at my head.

CHAPTER 5

OPEN

I felt something release in my chest. Like a lone glacier drifting away from a tundra. I knew right then that the bus driver had sealed my fate with his concurrence. Any slightest resistance that I might have posed against these brainless hooligans was dismissed by the authority of his opinion. Not that I necessarily planned on taking them all on by myself.

Yea—no, that'd be suicide.

But in moments of crippling weakness, when I sensed the boundless distance that sequestered me from the people of this country, I would reach out to my nostalgic memories of the life I knew back home. Until now, I thought this was the best possible action I could take. But thanks to them, I realized the futility of my actions, the futility of my memories, and the futility of my convictions.

I realized also that this independent realization constituted an act of betrayal to the people of my community. For the shame of selfhood in a culture that exists predominantly outside the creed of a foreign land can sometimes predispose an individual to assimilate into the ways beyond recognition. I was aware of this hypocrisy that loomed above my head for anyone inside and outside of my community to see. Yet, henceforth, I'd spend the rest of my days rationalizing this decision to myself and others.

So I took off my *kufi* cap.[3]

Placing it on the empty seat next to me, I looked around me. The bald man and the rest of the passengers now pointed at my chest.

My *thobe*? [4]

They nodded with one head.

I pulled the spotlessly white *thobe* off my body, folding it atop the *kufi* cap on the adjacent seat. I stood there wearing nothing but a white undershirt tucked into baggy white *sirwal* pants.[5]

Without looking up, I stripped down to my knee-length underwear. I discarded the white undershirt among the powdery dust motes under my seat. My *sirwal* pants lay wrangled over the pile of clothes.

I turned to the bald man. His index finger was aimed at the emergency exit window beside me. He mouthed, "*Open.*"

I understood at once.

Glancing back at the bus driver in the rearview mirror, who kept mouthing *Open*, I turned to face my fellow passengers. As if I expected them to reveal a contradictory opinion. They had their index fingers aimed at the emergency exit window, also mouthing *Open*.

I pulled the emergency exit window latch downwards. A sheet of glass dropped down. A current of humid air fluttered by the open window; it encouraged me to take the leap. I climbed out the window, see-sawing into the dusky morning like a loose sheet of paper.

Epilogue

As Y. ran towards the bus-stop at the end of the city block, he burst out laughing at the strangeness of his own situation.

Here he was on vacation in Chicago. He was rushing to catch the bus—for no particular reason, really, other than to make a date with someone he'd never even met before. She was his fiancé. They'd talked on the phone, maybe, a handful of times. He knew just a little more about her than the strangers who walked by him on the sidewalk.

And yet, by virtue of her presence in this foreign city, he was elbowing his way through a buzzing crowd, resolutely headed for a cafe somewhere in the downtown area.

Intently, he watched people lining up at the bus stop over the heads in the crowd. They were boarding the transit bus without pause. He mentally willed them to slow down, to give him a moment to file in line behind them.

But they just kept passing through those narrow bus doors, one after another, like frantic ants pinched by fire. He observed their silhouettes behind the tinted windows along the body of the bus, milling around the aisle, ultimately settling for the seats in the back, while the last stragglers to board filled the seats up front.

He was suddenly mortified to hear the doors hiss shut. *Oh, no!*

He bolted for the bus stop. But, by the time he reached it, the bus had already pulled away from the curb.

He gazed sadly at the rear tinted windows. He saw a few heads turn back to stare at him. Then, the bus's left blinker flashed a couple of times, as it merged into the traffic gently streaming down the boulevard.

He took a seat on a discolored oak bench. Next to him, a man in knee-length underwear dozed against one of the glass walls of the bus stop shelter. Y. didn't pay him much mind. Absently, he studied the unemotional faces of the people that flitted by them on the sidewalk.

What should he do?

He could order an Uber. He'd already ordered two since he'd landed in the airport: one that took him to his hotel, and another that dropped him off downtown. If he ordered another Uber, it would just get clogged in the annoying downtown traffic.

He couldn't be any later for the reservation—he just realized. Biting his fist, he imagined his fiancé already having arrived with her *mahram*[6], waiting for him on the rooftop of the Expat Cafe that overlooked the still azure waters of the Chicago River. She wouldn't call him to make sure of his arrival. No, she wasn't the type. She'd just get up and leave.

Out of boredom, he turned to look at the man in knee-length underwear beside him. What a city. Back in Abu Dhabi, they'd have this rascal arrested for public nudity.

"Don't," the man said under his breath, eyes closed.

Y. looked confused.

"Don't do it."

"You sbeak to me?" Y. said in broken English.

The man didn't even open his eyes. He just kept dozing as his knees curled up to his chest. Without missing a beat, he wrapped his arms around them, rocking back and forth on his end of the bench.

"Don't do it, brother."

"Don't do *wat?*"

"Don't get on the next bus."

"Why?"

The man said nothing.

Y. turned away from him, shaking his head.

Drugs.

He marveled at how completely and irrevocably they upended someone's life. One day, you were happy and optimistic about the sprouting possibilities of the future; and the next, you were swept away into a sordid life of addiction and dependency. All it took was one wrong turn...

Another bus pulled up to the curb.

Sighing in relief, Y. stood up. He lined up behind a group of people waiting to board the bus.

As he settled into a seat by the emergency exit window, he turned to look at the bus stop one last time. The man was already fast asleep. He felt like he couldn't take his eyes off him. He fascinated him in the way a terrible tragedy on the news keeps your eyes glued to the screen.

And that was when he felt a thousand eyes boring into him; but he didn't feel like looking around him just yet;

because a quiet little voice at the back of his head told him to savor his fading feeling of kinship with this stranger who dozed on the bench mere feet beyond the tinted glass, and yet, who already felt thousands of miles away.

Afterword

As formerly and presently colonized peoples around the world intimately know, the impact of colonization occurs outwardly in the material world as well as internally. While the former is destabilizing and marked by drastic changes to the land, it is the internal impacts that are most devastating. In Waseem Bahra's short story *On the Bus*, readers join the latest iteration of the postcolonial literary journey started decades ago.

On the Bus reflects themes and ideas similar to Sudanese writer Tayeb Salih in his postcolonial novel *Season of Migration to the North*.[1] Although decades apart, Salih and Bahra's literary contributions speak to each other about the layered impacts of colonization and ways to overcome them.

It is not just in literature but also in song that postcolonial themes are reflected. In the Palestinian-Jordanian singer Zeyne's introduction to the song *Asli Ana*,[2] she states, "They were pestering you about your thobe...They said people would laugh at us, and we should catch up with civilization." She continues with, "If I shed my thobe, I'll be shedding my very skin."

In *On the Bus*, readers join a nameless bus rider as he navigates a cultural landscape much different from his own. When he is targeted for his outward appearance—specifically, his thobe—he is faced with a familiar dilemma: assimilate or perish.

On the Bus effectively reflects on the spaces where we are no longer seen as individuals but rather as symbols of a larger cultural and political current. The short story challenges readers to reach a deeper understanding of the choices immigrants and refugees face in the mundane moments of daily life and how the consequence of those choices permeate into the core of identity and personhood.

Cultural identity is often showcased through outward appearance such as clothing and head coverings. For the protagonist of *On the Bus*, it is through his thobe and kufi cap. When he is forced to remove those items, he is also forced to remove his anchor (i.e. the main stabilizing force of his identity).

It becomes increasingly clear to readers that it is not just the thobe or the outward symbols of a culture that are removed, but the inner sources of identity that are also called into question and uprooted. To the protagonist, this is different from the occasional soul-searching that marks transitional phases of life. It is more like a violent unmaking that saps the marrow from the bone, a veritable hollowing out.

On the Bus addresses colonialism as a method of breeding social disconnect. While colonization and the extractive forces of capitalism carve deep craters into the hearts of the colonized, it simultaneously fails to fill those ever-growing craters with anything of substance. As a result, the colonized and the colonizer are ravenous for connection, forever trying to fill an emptiness which can never be satiated.

Bahra's bus is more than just a setting in the story. It is also an object of capitalistic, hyper-individualism synonymous with the West. Bahra writes, "They were boarding the transit bus without pause. He mentally willed them to slow down, to give him a moment to file in line behind them."[3] This moment is a metaphor for assimilation and social conformity. Immigrants must board the bus to survive but at the relentless pace of the colonizer.

In the same vein, as Salih notes, there is a steep price to assimilation. A Sudanese character who is educated in Britain is described as "a noble person whose mind was able to absorb Western civilization but it broke his heart."[4] This same heartbreak is showcased in the protagonist's internal dialogue when he states, "I felt something release in my chest. Like a lone glacier drifting away from a tundra."[5] Here the protagonist is speaking to the deep heartbreak that separation engenders in the colonized.

The economic, political, and social system of colonization rely on the idea of an "other" in order to function. This entails transforming people into objects or ideas and separating them from their personhood while extracting their labor and culture for the benefit of the Empire.

While referring to interactions with a British woman, the character in Salih's novel reflects that, "She gazed hard and long at me as though seeing me as a symbol rather than reality."[6] This sentiment is echoed by Bahra when he writes, "He was staring at me. His mouth dangled open, forming an O with his saltine-thin, chapped lips."[7] Soon, other passengers join in the outing of this immigrant "stranger", who is viewed as a symbol of foreignness and perhaps something more sinister rather than reality.

While indigenous ways of being are based in connection, wholeness, and deep-rooted relationship with the land and each other, under colonization everything is carved up piecemeal and separated. This fragmentation is often startling to newly arrived immigrants.

After coming face to face with the xenophobia on the bus, Bahra's character states, "I climbed out the window, see-sawing into the dusky morning like a loose sheet of paper."[8] This image is fitting because colonization separates bodies from the land and from each other, leaving them unmoored "like a loose sheet of paper."

Similarly, Salih's character faces dehumanization under the yoke of British control of Sudan. He resists it by saying, "No, I am not a stone thrown into the water but seed sown in a field."[9] The way that a seed's roots are nourished by soil in the field, indigenous people of the world over-depend on their deep connection to the land for nourishment.

This is why it is a form of resistance to refuse to see oneself as the stone—but to remain as the seed sown in the field.

Colonization depends on control of language as a way to exact control over the population. As Salih states, "The ships at first sailed down the Nile carrying guns not bread, and the railways were originally set up to transport troops; the schools were started so as to teach us how to say 'Yes' in their language."[10] It is the "Yes" colonization is after, the acquiesce and lack of resistance to the colonizer's will.

When Bahra's protagonist asks, "What happened to my voice?"[11] He is speaking to the way colonization has impacted his language and way of expressing himself. He continues reflecting that his voice "was normally very loud, especially if I refused someone something."[12]

Bahra's character finds that this refusal, the precious and holy "No" is suddenly not accessible to him in this place far from home, in this state as a colonized person far from freedom.

Bahra's short story concludes with a warning. The protagonist, now stripped of his identity and agency, encounters a new character who is also an immigrant at the bus stop. "Don't do it, brother," he says in hopes that this new character will make a different choice.[13] In *Season of Migration to the North*, Salih offers a similar warning when he states, "Were every person to know when to refrain from taking the first step, many things would have been changed."[14] When it comes to colonization, the first step cannot be avoided—only faced head on and resisted.

As the singer Zeyne notes, "If I shed my thobe, I'll be shedding my very skin." She offers us a perspective that values the thobe—or largely, the culture which the thobe represents. She is saying that if one were to keep their "skin" or sense of self, one must actively work to eradicate the colonizer within. There is no easy way to achieve this self-determination, particularly in the face of violent supremacy.

Salih offers up a form of resistance in this line when his character states, "If we are lies, we shall be lies of our own making."[15] This invocation of the "We" resists the "I" that colonization seeds. It encourages self-determination even if ever so imperfectly.

Bahra's story closes with a new character on the bus. He gazes out the emergency exit window and reflects on his encounter with the stranger at the bus stop. He feels the curse of forced assimilation closing in on him and thinks he ought to "savor his fading feeling of kinship with this stranger." It is as though part of him knows that it is only through shared kinship and connection that the curse can be lifted.

While readers are always encouraged to make their own meaning of a text, it is clear that *On the Bus* joins the postcolonial literary tradition. It calls in the classic themes of the genre while offering its own flavor for our ever-changing times, marking it as *the* must-read for our current moment.

Nada Samih-Rotondo
12/28/2024
Rhode Island

Notes

CHAPTER 1

1. a building used for public worship, religious activities, and learning by Muslims.

2. Similar to Sunday service for Christians, Friday prayer (or *Salah al-Jumu'ah* as it is known among Muslims) is a community prayer service held once a week on Fridays in which Muslim men engage in performing ablutions, prayer, and listening to a *khutbah* (i.e. sermon). Women and children may also participate, but they are not doctrinally obligated to.

CHAPTER 5

3. a round brimless cotton cap that serves as a material symbol of religiosity for some Muslim men.
4. a flowing long-sleeved, ankle-length gown-like kaftan worn by Muslim men during prayer and religious occasions.
5. loose-fitting pants with a wide crotch gusset that are typically worn under a thobe.

EPILOGUE

6. an adult male or female guardian who escorts a Muslim woman on a journey.

A F T E R W O R D

1. Salih, Tayeb. *Season of Migration to the North*. Cambridge eng.: Proquest LLC, 1991.

2. **'Asli Ana-** أصلي أنا'
   Words and Music by Giorgio Schipani, Kauner Michael, Qusai Sroor - قصي سرور, Ehab Qawasmi - إيهاب القواسمي, Nasir AlBashir - ناصر البشير, Yazan Rousan & zeyne - زين

3. Quoted in Bahra, *On the Bus, Epilogue*.
4. Quoted in Salih, *Season of Migration to the North, 9*.
5. Quoted in Bahra, *On the Bus, Chapter 5*.
6. Quoted in Salih, *Season of Migration to the North, 28*.
7. Quoted in Bahra, *On the Bus, Chapter 3*.
8. Quoted in Bahra, *On the Bus, Chapter 5*.
9. Quoted in Salih, *Season of Migration to the North, 6*.
10. Quoted in Salih, *Season of Migration to the North, 79*.
11. Quoted in Bahra, *On the Bus, Chapter 4*.
12. Quoted in Bahra, *On the Bus, Chapter 4*.
13. Quoted in Bahra, *On the Bus, Epilogue*.
14. Quoted in Salih, *Season of Migration to the North, 5*.
15. Quoted in Salih, *Season of Migration to the North, 49-50*.

Acknowledgments

I would like to extend my deepest gratitude to Dr. Nicolai N. Petro of the University of Rhode Island for his edits.

A very big thank you to everyone at the Bahra Books team for being unconditionally supportive and unapologetically goofy throughout this wonderful journey. Without you, this book would not have seen the light of day.

My gratitude to Nada Samih-Rotondo for the phenomenal job she did on the 'Afterword'.

Istvan! Lana! Beautiful work on the book design.

We can't forget the flexible rock and also my brothers for being a constant in the marathon of fluctuations. That includes you, too, Ahmad Sirougie.

I can never thank my mother enough for birthing me—
الله المستعان عليك يا ابني.

And, of course, my father for making me the man I am.

Lastly, I would like to dedicate this first short story to Ms. Robidoux, the first believer. Wherever you are, I hope you know you made one boy's dream another man's reality.

BAHRA BOOKS

ON THE BUS

Book Club Guide

Reading Group
Discussion Questions

Book Club
Conversation Starters

More Books Like
On the Bus

DISCUSSION QUESTIONS

1. The story begins with the unnamed protagonist self-consciously observing the reluctant behavior of the people around him. How does his self-consciousness set the stage for the ending of the short story?

2. Clothing plays an important role in the book, such as the protagonist's thobe and kufi. What purpose do you think the description of clothing serves in the short story?

3. We never enter the minds of any other characters in the book. If you could hear the thoughts of the passengers, what do you think they would say about the protagonist?

4. The protagonist's relationship with his culture seems complicated. How does his complicated relationship with culture determine the fate of his journey, both literally and metaphorically?

5. The bus serves as a confined space where the protagonist cannot escape his thoughts nor surroundings. What might the bus symbolize in the story?

6. In the epilogue, we are introduced to Y., a fellow traveler from Abu Dhabi. What role does he play in the story? How does his own bus ride enhance the thematic narrative?

7. The protagonist claims to feel like an outsider in the city and to harbor mixed feelings about its inhabitants. How do his convictions shape his internal monologue? Do you find his perspective justified or unreasonable?

8. While the purpose of Y.'s bus ride is to meet up with his fiancé, the reason why the protagonist's on the bus remains unclear. Where do you think he's going? Why is he in such a rush?

9. The author has said he was reading a lot of Kafka while writing *On the Bus*. Are there any other influences you can spot?

10. What do you think happens at the end of the book? It leaves off at a cliffhanger of sorts.

BOOK CLUB
CONVERSATION STARTERS

CAUTION, SPOILERS AHEAD!

"What do you think the protagonist's decision to 'rely on his instincts' rather than technology suggests about his character and his approach to navigating unfamiliar spaces?"

Discuss how this choice reflects deeper themes of trust, self-reliance, and resistance to modernity.

"The protagonist perceives a strong social rejection from the people he encounters. How does this perception shape his internal dialogue?"

Explore the psychological impact that the protagonist's experiences have on his interpretations of others' behavior.

"The protagonist's critique of the locals sharply contrasts with his outward silence on the bus. What does this tension reveal about his identity and values?"

Delve into the paradox between the protagonist's internal judgments and his outward actions.

"What role do the fleeting observations of other passengers play in building the atmosphere of the bus scene? How does this contribute to the passenger's isolation?"

Analyze how small details (like seating choices and body language) create a sense of unease or detachment.

"The protagonist questions, 'Am I wrong not to love them?' How does this moment complicate the reader's understanding of his feelings toward the locals?"

Discuss the complexity of the protagonist's emotions, oscillating between disdain, empathy, and self-doubt.

MORE BOOKS LIKE
ON THE BUS

SEASON OF MIGRATION *by* Tayeb Salih

After years of study in Europe, the young narrator of *Season of Migration to the North* returns to his village along the Nile in the Sudan. It is the 1960s, and he is eager to make a contribution to the new postcolonial life of his country. Back home, he discovers a stranger among the familiar faces of childhood—the enigmatic Mustafa Sa'eed. Mustafa takes the young man into his confidence, telling him the story of his own years in London, of his brilliant career as an economist, and of the series of fraught and deadly relationships with European women that led to a terrible public reckoning and his return to his native land. But what is the meaning of Mustafa's shocking confession? Mustafa disappears without explanation, leaving the young man—whom he has asked to look after his wife—in an unsettled and violent no-man's-land between Europe and Africa, tradition and innovation, and man and woman, from which no one will escape unaltered or unharmed.

BREAKING KNEES *by* Zakria Tamer

The first of Zakaria Tamer's collections of stories to be published in English as one volume, *Breaking Knees* is a daring work of art that deals with taboo subjects like authority and freedom in a direct manner. Many stories stress the dominance of cultural institutions and conventions that constrain individual decisions. Wry, satirical and bawdy, Tamer's stories are imbued with glimpses of the corrupt, fearful lives citizens lead under a violent dictatorship in Syria.

THE MADMAN *by* Khalil Gibran

Thought-provoking and inspiring, *The Madman* is a collection of memorable parables and poems, many of them casting an ironic light on the beliefs, aspirations, and vanities of humankind. Among the 35 poems and parables in this volume are "How I Became a Madman," "The Two Hermits," "The Wise Dog," "Night and the Madman," "The Three Ants," "When My Sorrow Was Born," "And When My Joy Was Born," among others. Kahlil Gibran first became known to Americans in 1918 with the publication of this book.

BAHRA BOOKS

About the Author

Born in Providence, Rhode Island, Waseem Bahra spent his childhood in the ancient capital of Damascus. He started writing when he relocated to the States in 2013 after the outbreak of the Syrian Civil War. He has been published under a pseudonym in the following journals, periodicals, and magazines: Meniscus Literary Journal, The Dead Mule School of Southern Literature, Arabica Journal, Poet's Choice Magazine, among others. *On the Bus* is his first short story.

www.bahrabooks.com

@bahrabooks

BAHRA BOOKS

Founded in 2024, Bahra Books publishes a highly curated selection of five titles a year. The selection consists of both fiction and nonfiction. They accept submissions for consideration through their official website: www.bahrabooks.com.

www.ingramcontent.com/pod-product-compliance
Lightning Source LLC
Chambersburg PA
CBHW020607130626
46552CB00007B/3093